SUPER STARS!
ADDING & SUBTRACTING
Activity Book

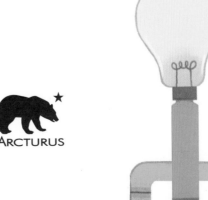

ARCTURUS

ARCTURUS

This edition published in 2019 by Arcturus Publishing Limited
26/27 Bickels Yard, 151–153 Bermondsey Street,
London SE1 3HA

Written by Lorenzo McLellan
Illustrated by Natasha Rimmington
Designed by Well Nice
Edited by Sebastian Rydberg

ISBN: 978-1-78828-597-1
CH006145NT
Supplier 29, Date 0219, Print run 7924

Printed in China

How to Use This Book

Welcome to the world of Super Stars! This book is filled with number facts to help you learn the basics of adding and subtracting—all while having fun!

Read about each new topic before you dive in to the activities.

Test your knowledge with fun activities throughout.

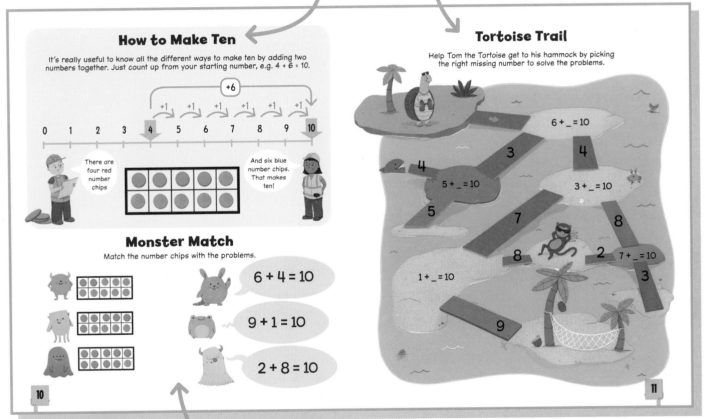

How to Make Ten

It's really useful to know all the different ways to make ten by adding two numbers together. Just count up from your starting number, e.g. 4 + 6 = 10.

There are four red number chips

And six blue number chips. That makes ten!

Monster Match

Match the number chips with the problems.

6 + 4 = 10

9 + 1 = 10

2 + 8 = 10

10

Tortoise Trail

Help Tom the Tortoise get to his hammock by picking the right missing number to solve the problems.

6 + _ = 10

3

4

4

5 + _ = 10

3 + _ = 10

5

7

8

8

2

7 + _ = 10

1 + _ = 10

3

9

11

All new topics come with practice activities to learn key skills.

Numbers

First off, let's see if you can recognize numbers all the way from 1 to 100.

Nonsense Numbers

Can you spot which monkeys have made-up numbers?

Brick Fix

Help finish building the wall by filling in the holes with the right order of bricks.

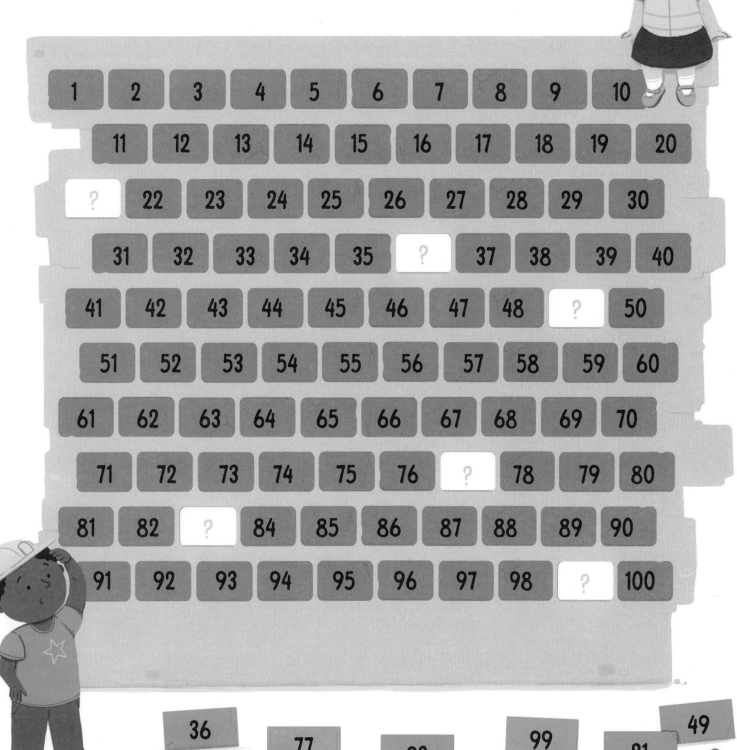

Symbols (+ - =)

Each symbol means something different.

MEANS "ADD" **MEANS "SUBTRACT"** **MEANS "IS EQUAL TO"**

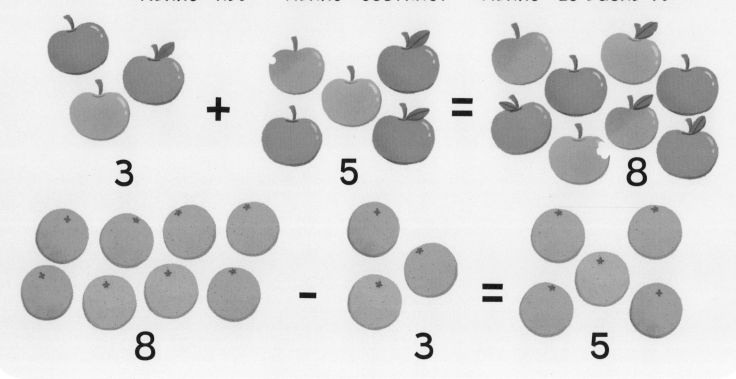

$$3 + 5 = 8$$

$$8 - 3 = 5$$

Seal Surprise

Which symbol is each seal hiding? Fill in the answer, choosing between +, -, or =.

$$2 + 3 \quad \_\_\_ \quad 5$$

$$5 \quad \_\_\_ \quad 6 = 11$$

$$6 \quad \_\_\_ \quad 2 = 4$$

$$20 \quad \_\_\_ \quad 10 + 10$$

Jungle Jumble

Oh no! The mischievous monkeys have mixed up some of the symbols.
Can you spot which four symbols are wrong?

$2 + 12 = 14$

$4 - 6 = 10$

$20 + 30 = 50$

$10 - 5 = 15$

$7 - 3 = 10$

$20 + 5 = 15$

$13 + 8 = 21$

Magic Mix-up

The magician has dropped all his cards! Add up the numbers on each card to find the total. Write the totals in order, from smallest to largest.

9+3 16+7 6+5 8+9

SMALLEST | ? | ? | ? | ? | LARGEST

Seashell Surprise

Which mermaid has won the golden shell?
Circle the problem that is equal to the number of the shell.

15

8+9   15+5   4+5   7+8

Penguin Panic

Guide the chick across the ice to reach home!
Solve the problems, and shade in the answers.

START HERE

8+9

17

5+7

12

10+9

15

16

23

19

20

25+5

16+6

15+5

9

22

7+8

12

15

5+5

10

HOME

How to Make Ten

It's really useful to know all the different ways to make ten by adding two numbers together. Just count up from your starting number, e.g. 4 + 6 = 10.

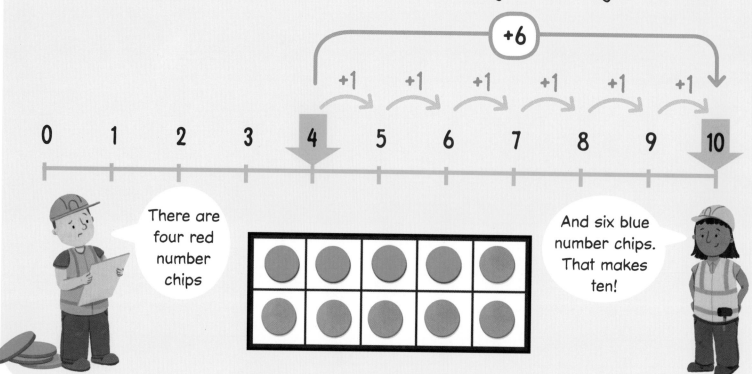

There are four red number chips

And six blue number chips. That makes ten!

Monster Match

Match the number chips with the problems.

 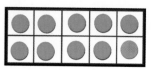

 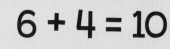
$$6 + 4 = 10$$

$$9 + 1 = 10$$

$$2 + 8 = 10$$

Tortoise Trail

Help Tom the Tortoise get to his hammock by picking the right missing number to solve the problems.

$6 + \_ = 10$

3

4

4

$5 + \_ = 10$

$3 + \_ = 10$

5

7

8

8

2

$7 + \_ = 10$

$1 + \_ = 10$

3

9

Wild, Wild West

Pair up the horses and cowboys to make 10.

Under the Sea

Which numbers are the fish hiding?

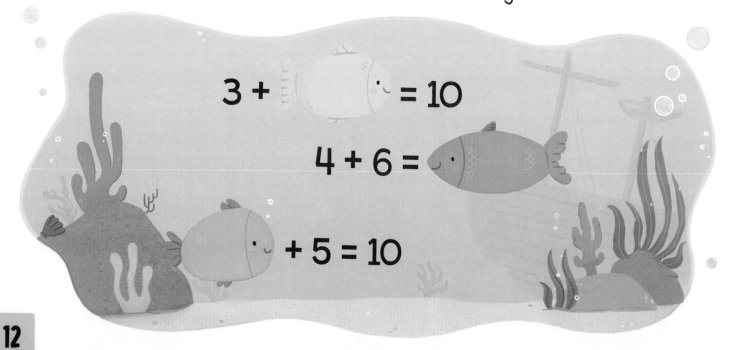

$$3 + = 10$$

$$4 + 6 = $$

$$ + 5 = 10$$

Robo-road

Help the robot collect the tools and get back to his friends.
You can only pick roads that add up to 10.

How to Make Twenty

Now let's add two numbers to make twenty, e.g. 14 + 6 = 20.

0   1   2   3   4   5   6   7   8   9

+6

+1 +1 +1 +1 +1 +1

10   11   12   13   14   15   16   17   18   19   20

Pixie Party

Which numbers are the pixies hiding?

2 + 🧚 = 10

4 + 🧚 = 10

9 + 🧚 = 20

5 + 5 = 🧚

🧚 + 3 = 20

0 + 🧚 = 20

14

Superhero Sort Out

Can you match the superheroes together to make 20?

Find the Treasure

The treasure is in the chest with the correct sum. Which one is it?

14 + 4 = 20

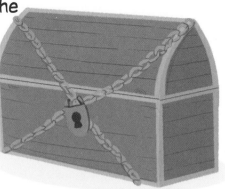

13 + 6 = 20

18 + 2 = 20

Dino-roar

Which number does each dinosaur need to make 20? Write your answer in the blank provided.

15 _

19 _

14 _

8 _

7 _

Safari Sun

Look at the sum in the sun. Which animal has the correct answer?

13 + 6 =

17

20

19

Knight Time!

Shade in the knight's shield by solving the problems in the key.

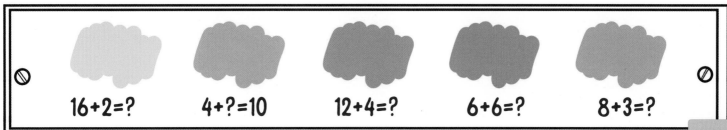

16+2=?   4+?=10   12+4=?   6+6=?   8+3=?

Test Your Knowledge

What are the ice caps and islands hiding?

$4 \; ? \; 6 = 10$

$2 \; ? \; 7 = 9$

$1 \; ? \; 4 = 5$

$5 + 6 = \; ?$

$6 + 6 = \; ?$

$7 + 5 = \; ?$

$8 + 8 = \; ?$

$11 + 9 = \; ?$

$12 + 8 = \; ?$

$13 + 7 = \; ?$

Test Your Knowledge

What's behind the card each monkey is hiding?

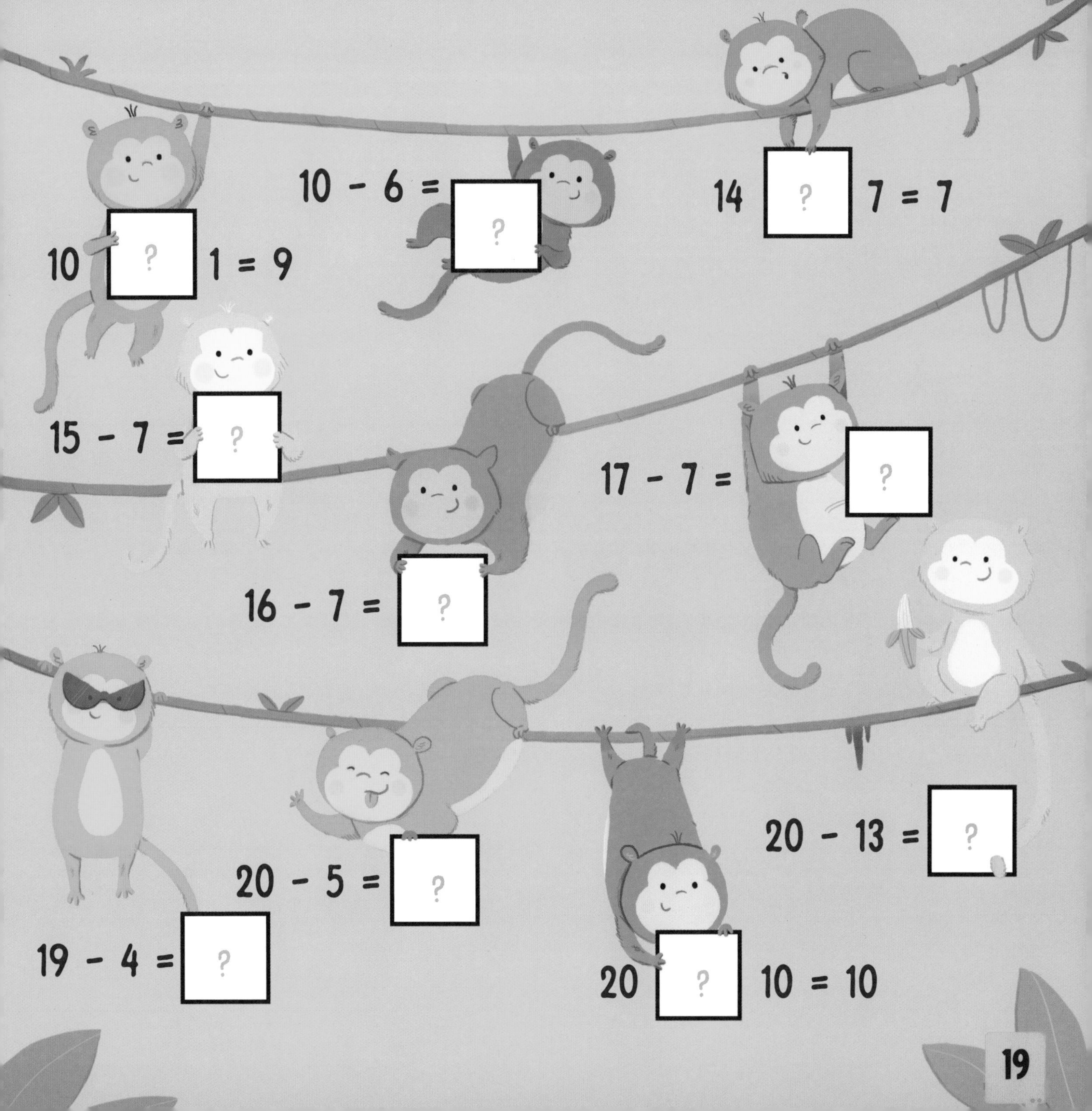

10 − 6 = ?

14 ? 7 = 7

10 ? 1 = 9

15 − 7 = ?

17 − 7 = ?

16 − 7 = ?

20 − 5 = ?

20 − 13 = ?

19 − 4 = ?

20 ? 10 = 10

How to Add 10

When adding 10, the digit in the ones column doesn't change, e.g. 12 + 10 = 22.

Balloon Brigade

Which numbers in the sequence are covered by clouds?

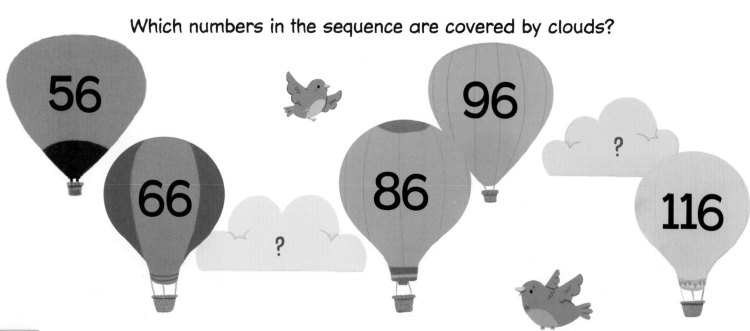

Egg Run

Help the chicken put her eggs in the right order.

Hop to It!

Work out the missing numbers on the lily pads to help the frog get to the other side of the pond.

Lost in Space

Guide each alien to their home planet by adding 10 to each ship.

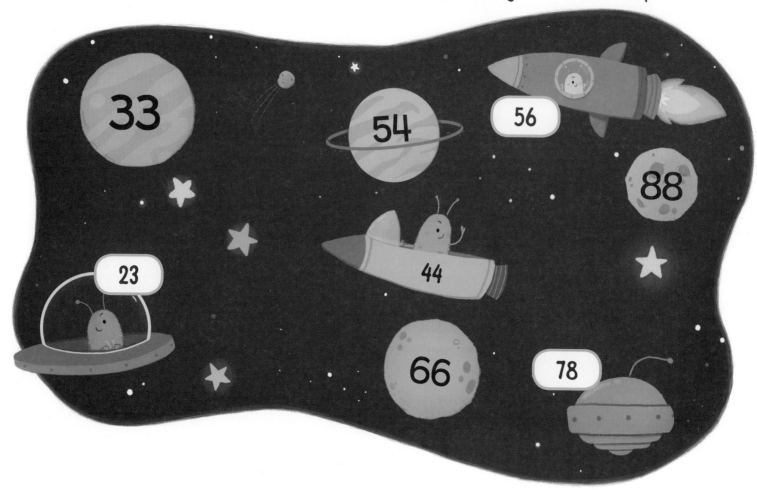

Fox Cub Club

Add all the cubs' numbers together to work out the answer.

The Highest Heights!

Work out the missing numbers on the mountains to get to the purple flag.

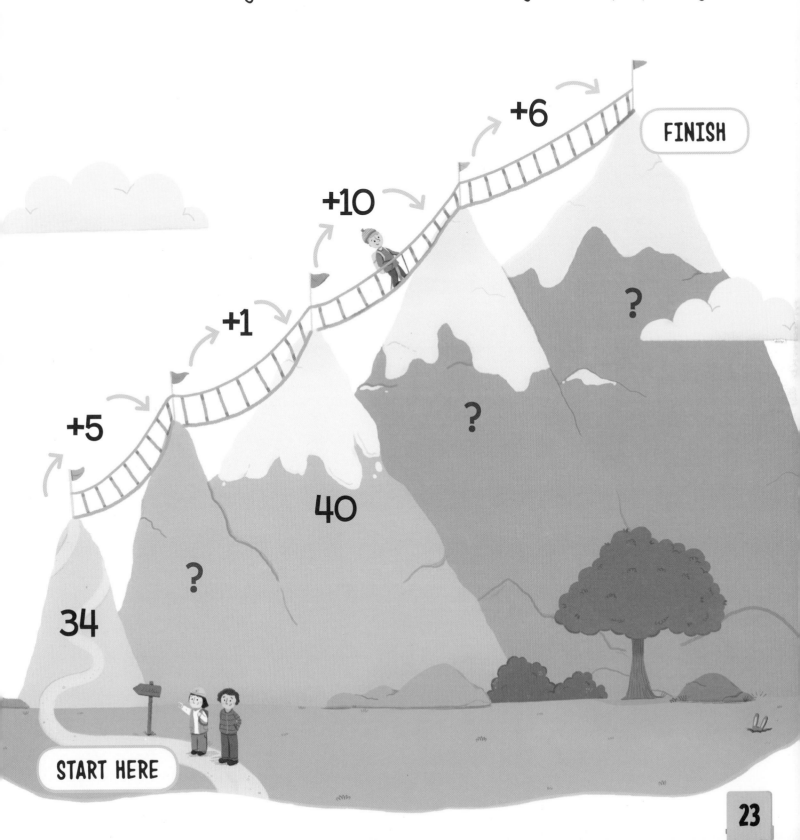

+6

FINISH

+10

?

+1

?

+5

40

34

?

START HERE

How to Add Multiples of 10

This time we are simply adding numbers in the ten times table,
e.g. 10 + 20 = 30, 43 + 30 = 73.

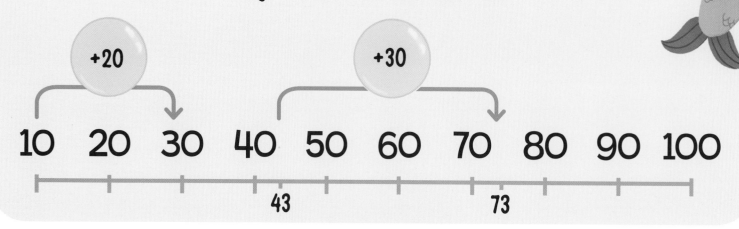

Fire Fight!

You need thirty more buckets of water to put out each fire.
Can you complete the number sentences?

22 + 30 = ?   69 + 30 = ?

Bubble Trouble

Match the fish and the bubbles to make three number sentences.

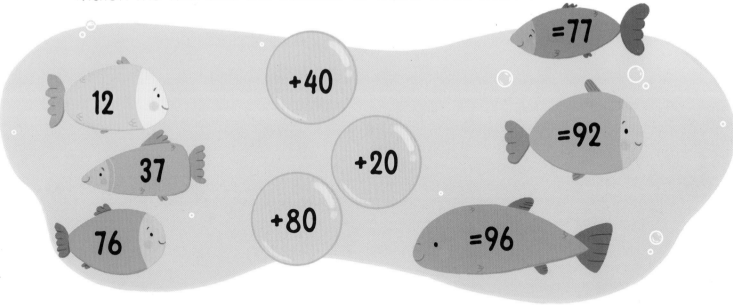

Pyramid Puzzle

Add up the bricks next to each other and write the total on the brick above them.

Super Supper

Look at the answer in the chef's hat.
Which superhero has the correct problem?

Fruit Salad

Add the numbers on the fruits together to get the answer.

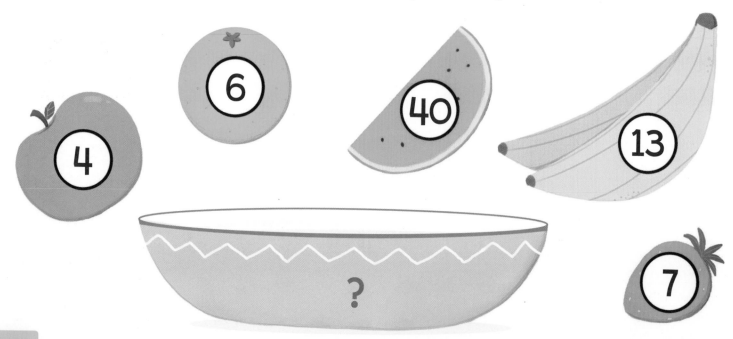

Deep Sea Diving

Solve the problems below, and then use the key to help you shade in the sea creatures.

18+10=?

37+40=?

12+30=?

16+4=?

8+80=?

How to Subtract 10

Now let's try taking 10 away—remember that the digit in the ones column doesn't change.

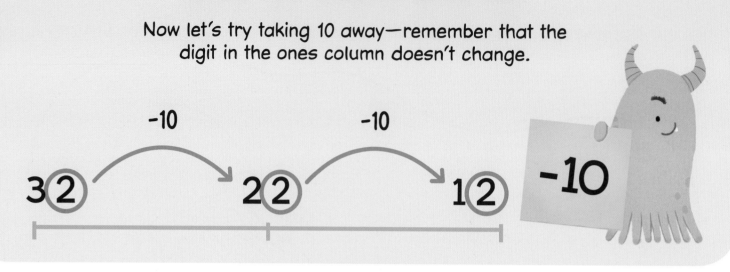

Pirate Plank

Subtract 10 each time to complete the sequence.

| 66 | 56 | ? | 36 | ? | ? |

Penguin Panic!

Help the penguin get home by subtracting 10 each time.

START HERE

55

45

34

23

35

25

10

15

HOME

29

Pick a Pride

Which lion belongs to the pride?
Solve the problems to find out!

67

77-10   87-10   97-10

Monkey Puzzle Trees

These monkeys are trying to make two number sentences. Can you help them?

67   =57   -10   47   =27   -20

Mummy's Secret

Solve the subtractions using the symbols key on the left.
Write the answer down to open the sarcophagus.

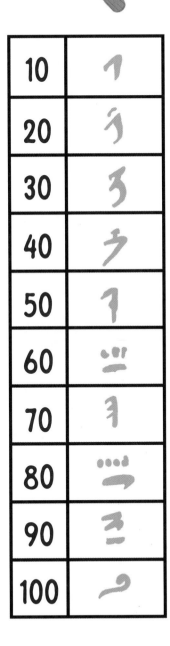

10	𝟣
20	𝟥
30	𝟥
40	𝟥
50	𝟣
60	ᵘᵘ
70	𝟥
80	⁝⁝
90	ᗒ
100	ᒿ

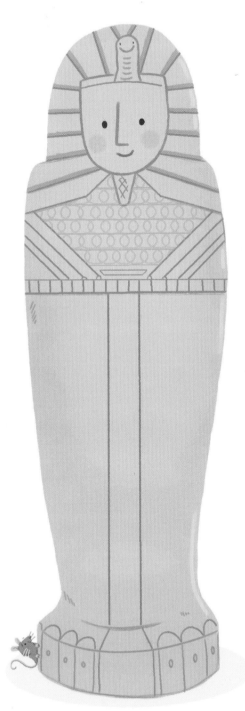

1) ⁝⁝ − 𝟥 = [?]

2) 𝟥 − 𝟣 = [?]

3) ᗒ − 𝟥 = [?]

How to Subtract Multiples of 10

Now you're ready to start taking away numbers in the ten times tables, e.g. 96 - 40 = 56, 43 - 20 = 23.

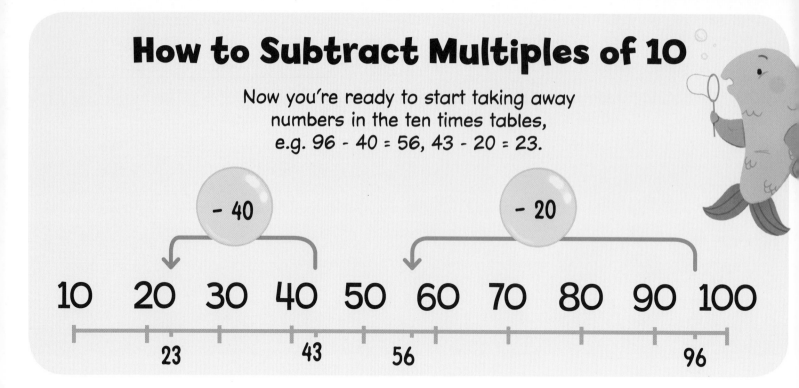

Pyramid Puzzle

Subtract the bricks next to each other and write the answer beneath them.

Balloon Brigade

Which numbers are missing from the balloons?

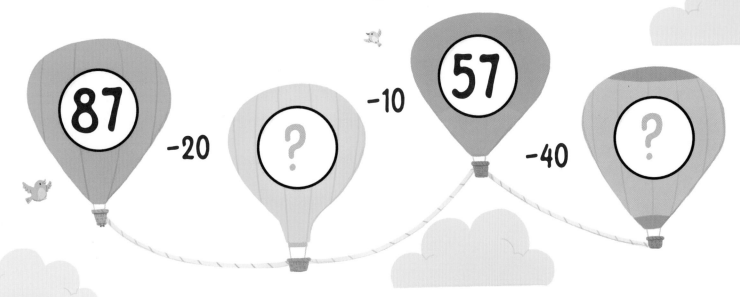

Superhero Sort Out

Link the superheroes and the explosions to make three number sentences.

Dino Dance

Help the dinosaur pick the right dance partner by solving the problem.

Super Save

Enter the solution to each problem to crack the code and free the superheroes!

Back to Base Camp

Work out the missing numbers on the mountain to help the climbers get back to camp.

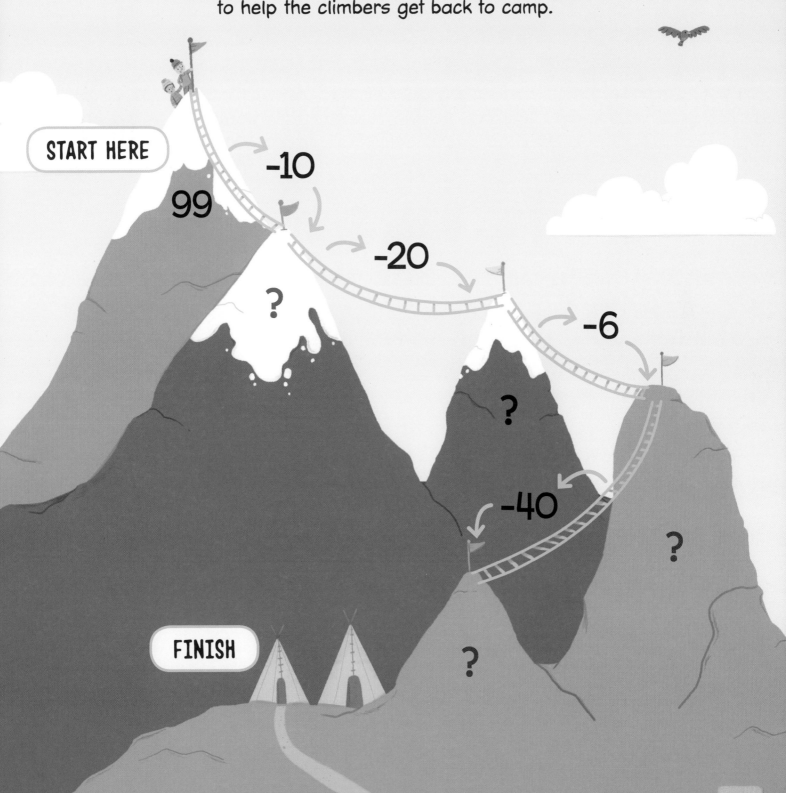

START HERE

99

-10

-20

?

-6

?

-40

?

?

?

FINISH

Test Your Knowledge

Complete the number sentences.

1) 1 + 10 = ?

2) 10 + 10 = ?

3) 20 + 20 = ?

4) 20 + 30 = ?

5) 33 + 10 = ?

6) 45 + 20 = ?

7) 65 + 30 = ?

8) 89 + 10 = ?

9) 24 + 70 = ?

10) 10 + 90 = ?

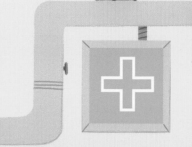

Test Your Knowledge

Complete the number sentences.

1) 11 - 10 = ❓

2) 20 - 10 = ❓

3) 30 - 10 = ❓

4) 50 - 10 = ❓

5) 53 - 10 = ❓

6) 60 - 30 = ❓

7) 84 - 40 = ❓

8) 99 - 90 = ❓

9) 87 - 60 = ❓

10) 33 - 30 = ❓

How to Add Ones and Tens

Add the ones first, next add the tens, and then add everything together.

START HERE

Step 1

3 + 5 = 8

Step 2

20 + 40 = 60

23 + 45

Step 3

60 + 8

= 68

Juggle Off

Find each juggler's missing number by adding their other two numbers together.

Space Stations

Solve the problem to send the spaceship to the right station.

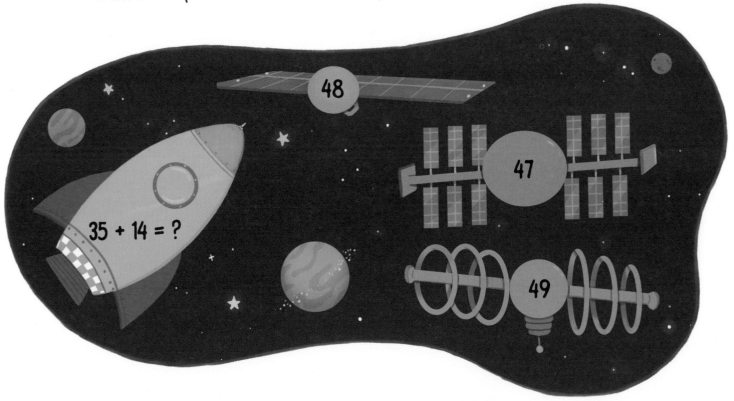

Tortoise Trouble

Match the tortoises with their shells.

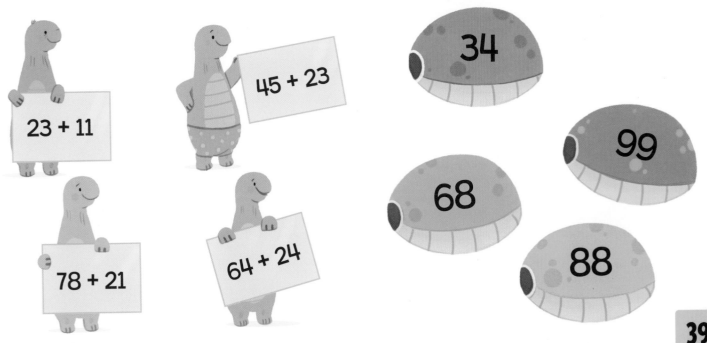

Mermaid Mystery

Which number sentence below equals the one in the shell?

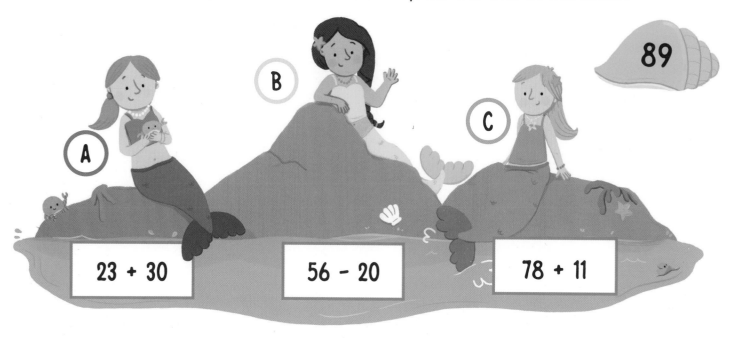

89

A
23 + 30

B
56 − 20

C
78 + 11

Seal Surprise

Which numbers are the seals hiding? Fill in the answers!

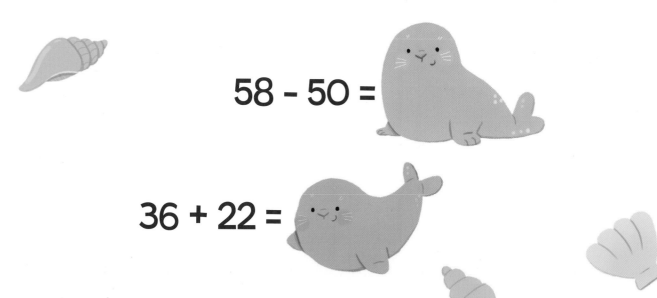

58 − 50 =

36 + 22 =

Dragon's Den

Shade in each part of the picture. Solve the problems and use the key to help you.

3+17=?   100-30=?   36+22=?   72-31=?   29-21=?

Banana Bonanza

How many bananas does the monkey have?

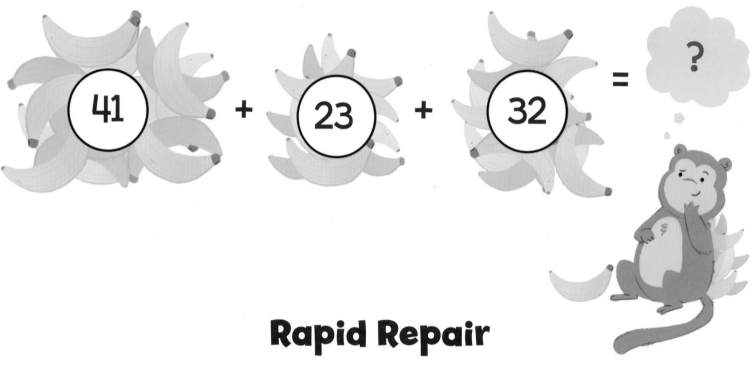

$41 + 23 + 32 = ?$

Rapid Repair

Fix the wall by picking the right bricks to complete each number sentence.

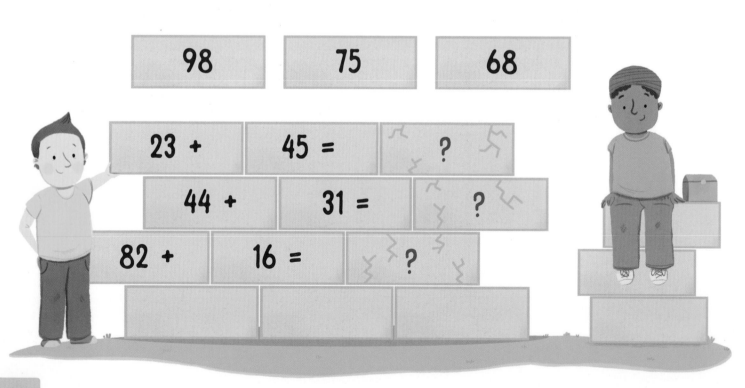

98   75   68

23 +   45 =   ?

44 +   31 =   ?

82 +   16 =   ?

Crack the Castle

Lower the bridge by working out the magic password.
Each answer will reveal a letter in the word.
There are more letters than needed in the key: don't be tricked!

P _ _ _ _ E
  5 4 3 2

1) 32 + 15 = 47

2) 46 + 23 = __

3) 82 + 16 = __

4) 16 + 73 = __

5) 36 + 63 = __

KEY

69 = S

89 = E

98 = A

99 = L

47 = U

67 = J

How to Subtract Ones and Tens

Subtract the ones first, next subtract the tens, and then add the answers together.

START HERE

Step 1

6 – 5 = 1

Step 2

50 – 20 = 30

56 – 25

Step 3

30 + 1

= 31

Picky Princess

Help the princess find the correct box for her shoes by matching it with the price tag.

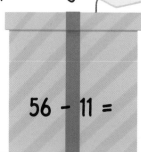

45

23 – 12 =

A

77 – 22 =

B

56 – 11 =

C

Pirate Puzzle

Draw lines to match each key to the right treasure chest.

65 – 41

84 – 23

97 – 81

16

61

24

Jungle Jumble

Those naughty monkeys have done it again!
Rearrange the answers so they are in the right place.

62 – 41 =   16

86 – 42 =   21

59 – 43 =   44

45

Search and Rescue

Help the foxes pick the right hole to find their cub.

68 - 41 =

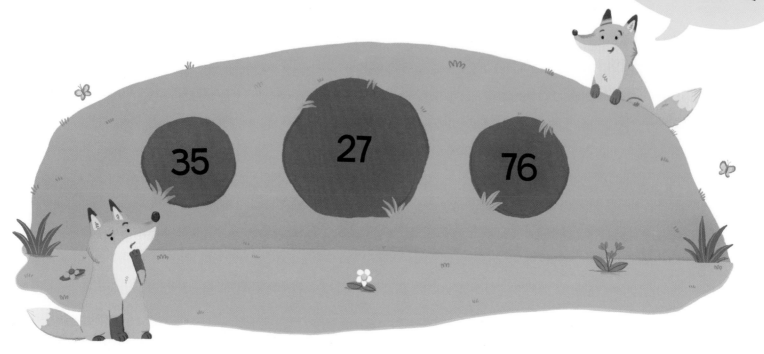

35

27

76

Bubble Burst

Which numbers are the bubbles hiding?

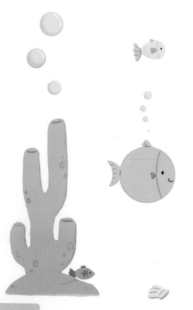

26 + 40 = ?

76 - 45 = ?

21 + 78 = ?

Mountain Maze

Climb to the highest peak. Follow the answers to the number sentences.

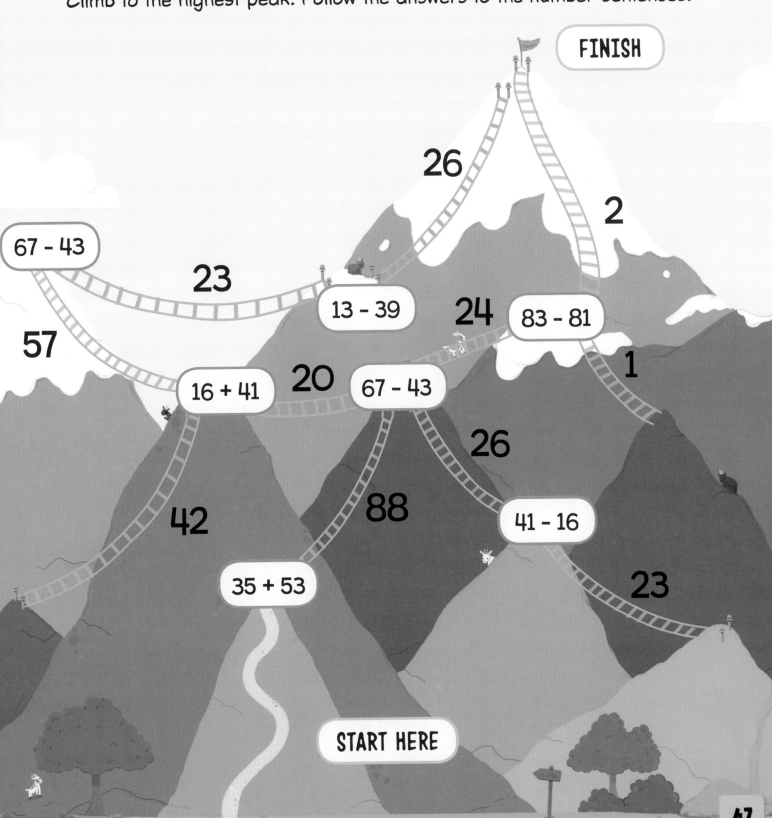

FINISH

26

2

67 – 43

23

13 – 39

24

83 – 81

57

1

16 + 41

20

67 – 43

42

26

88

41 – 16

35 + 53

23

START HERE

Safari Supper

Draw lines to match the food to the right animal.

$$34 - 23 =$$

$$67 - 45 =$$

$$98 - 63 =$$

11

35

22

Treasure Hunt

Which cave will lead to the treasure?

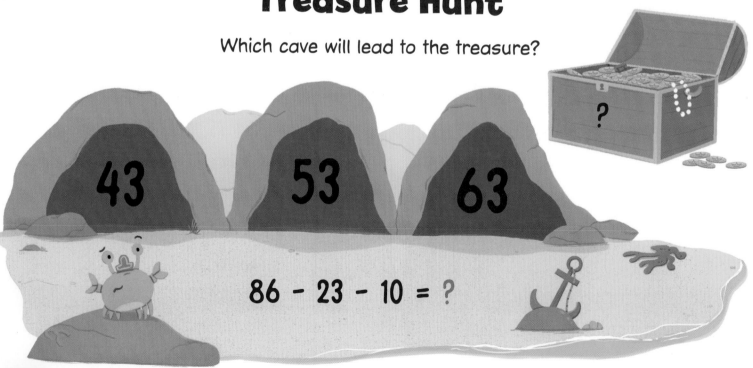

43

53

63

$$86 - 23 - 10 = ?$$

Crack the Code

Can you work out the word to open up the chest?
There are more letters than needed in the key: don't be tricked!

		B			E
1	2		3	4	

1) 35 + 10 = __

2) 67 − 10 = __

3) 45 + 24 = __

4) 11 + 82 = __

KEY

93 = L   45 = N

57 = I   68 = O

69 = B

Test Your Knowledge

Complete the number sentences.

1) 8 + [?] = 20

6) 58 – 10 = [?]

2) 20 + 40 = [?]

7) 4 + [?] = 10

3) 45 + 21 = [?]

8) [?] + 5 = 10

4) 80 – 60 = [?]

9) 13 + 7 = [?]

5) 37 + 22 = [?]

10) 89 – 80 = [?]

50

Test Your Knowledge

Complete the number sentences.

1) 36 + 32 = [?]

2) 56 + 32 = [?]

3) 88 - 32 = [?]

4) 67 - 45 = [?]

5) 74 - 63 = [?]

6) 99 - 79 = [?]

7) 35 + 44 = [?]

8) 75 + 21 = [?]

9) 75 - 21 = [?]

10) 84 - 84 = [?]

Doubling

Doubling is when you have two lots of the same number.

? + 3 3

WHAT IS DOUBLE **3** ?

3 + 3 = 6

Hop the Hurdles

The number on each hurdle is double the one before.
Work out the missing numbers.

A **2**

B ?

C ?

Washing Work Out

Find out which number goes on each basket.

3 + 3

12 + 12

24 + 24

? ? ?

Goblin Gold

Match each goblin to his bag of gold by doubling.

11

34

43

68

22

86

Bingo!

Can you find three number sentences in a row or column that give the same answer?

23 + 10	73 - 30	94 - 23
55 - 20	55 - 12	61 + 10
60 - 33	33 + 10	40 + 30

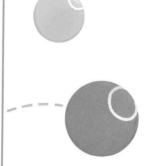

Pixie Party

Subtract 21 from each number in the sequence to find out what the missing numbers are.

Showtime

Help the clown get to the tent in time for the circus show!

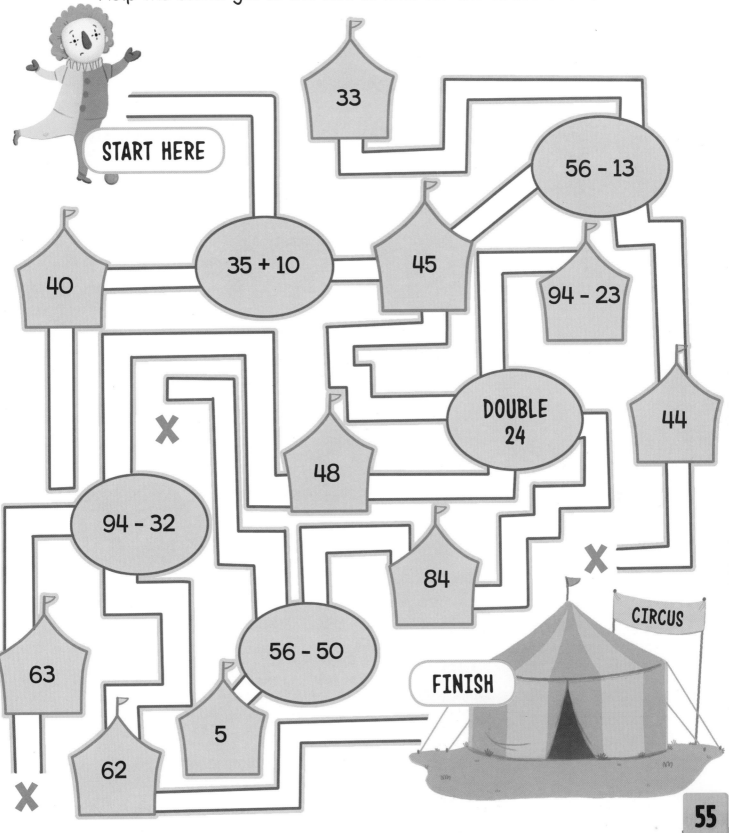

Bug Trail

Work out the missing numbers.

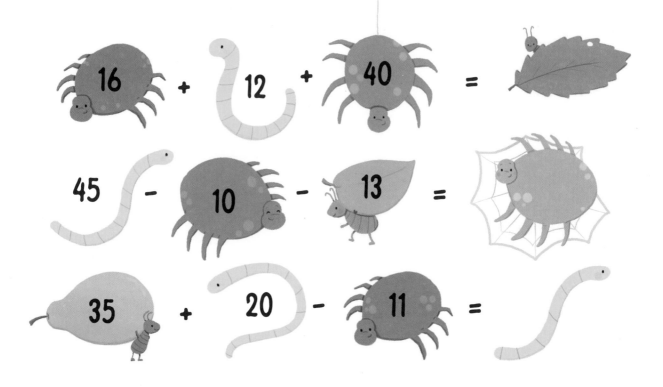

$16 + 12 + 40 =$

$45 - 10 - 13 =$

$35 + 20 - 11 =$

Pirate Picnic

Feed the pirates their preferred food. Draw a line to match the cards with the right answer.

$65 + 24$

$82 - 11$

$90 - 70$

71

89

20

Underwater Wonder

Which word are the fish trying to spell?
Remember, not all the letters in the key are needed!

1) 4 + 5 + 11 = __ 4) 57 - 16 = __ 67 = M 55 = A

2) 20 - 19 = __ 5) 20 + 30 + 17 = __ 20 = W 41 = O

3) 62 - 30 - 11 = __ 21 = C 1 = L

Missing Numbers

To work out the missing numbers on these pages, you will need to juggle the numbers and maybe switch the symbol.

1) If it helps, you could build a bar model.

$$2 + ? = 6$$

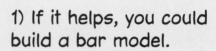

6	
2	?

$$6 - 2 = ?$$

2) Work out your new number sentence after switching the symbol.

$$6 - 2 = 4$$

Hard Hats On

First, rewrite the number sentences so that the missing number is at the end. The first one has been done for you. Then, work out the missing numbers.

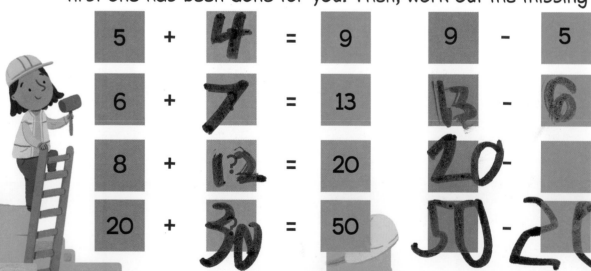

$$5 + 4 = 9 \qquad 9 - 5 = 4$$

$$6 + 7 = 13 \qquad 13 - 6 = 7$$

$$8 + 12 = 20 \qquad 20 - 8 = 12$$

$$20 + 30 = 50 \qquad 50 - 20 = 30$$

Balloon Brigade

Work out the missing numbers hidden by the clouds.

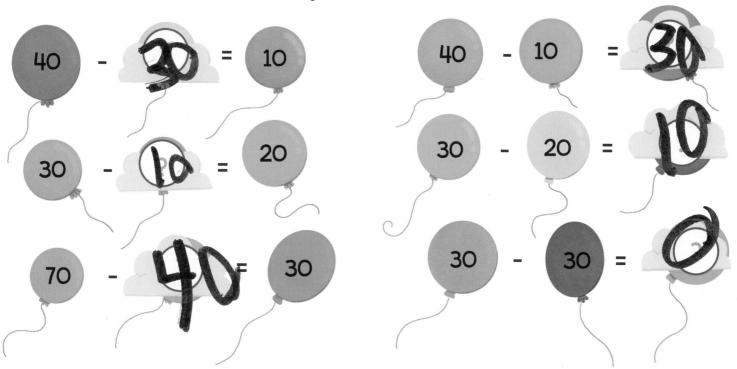

$40 - 30 = 10$

$30 - 10 = 20$

$70 - 40 = 30$

$40 - 10 = 30$

$30 - 20 = 10$

$30 - 30 = 0$

Robot Machines

Fill in the blank and work out the missing number.

$45 + 11 = 56$

$56 - 45 = ?$

Into the Wild

Which number is each animal hiding?

9 +  = 66

50 - 🦁 = 30

14 + 🐘 = 48

Wash Out

Which number completes the number sentence on the washing line?

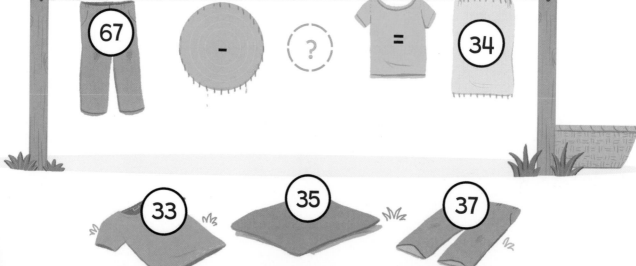

67   -   ?   =   34

33   35   37

Pirate Portrait

Solve the key and use it to help you shade in the pirate.

10 + ? = 50

10 + ? = 30

14 + ? = 46

74 - ? = 24

96 - ? = 34

Goblin Grab

Which number have the goblins taken?

$$67 - 15 = 52$$

(handwritten) 67 − 52 = (15)

Fairyland

Help the fairy to the castle by finding the missing number.

$$46 + ? = 99$$

(handwritten) + 51 / 46 / 197

(handwritten) 46

(handwritten) 48

(handwritten) 99 − 46 = 53

51   52   53

Mermaid Mystery

Can you crack the mermaid's secret message?

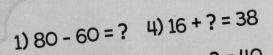

1) 80 – 60 = ?   4) 16 + ? = 38

2) 45 + 34 = ?   5) 49 – ? = 40

3) 76 – ? = 46   6) 49 – ? = 30

KEY

20 = J   22 = U

79 = N   9 = D

30 = M   19 = S

31 = T

Test Your Knowledge

Complete the number sentences.

1) 6 + 20 = ?

2) 5 + 15 = ?

3) 63 − 30 = ?

4) 35 + 30 = ?

5) 85 − 31 = ?

6) 92 − 90 = ?

7) 45 + 51 = ?

8) 76 − 35 = ?

9) 26 + 62 = ?

10) 75 − 71 = ?

Test Your Knowledge

Complete the number sentences.

1) 6 + **?** = 10

2) 14 + **?** = 20

3) 10 - **?** = 2

4) 20 - **?** = 9

5) 30 + **?** = 70

6) 90 - **?** = 10

7) 45 + **?** = 77

8) 43 - **?** = 31

9) 10 + **?** = 99

10) 99 - **?** = 10

How to Make 100

Jump up to the next multiple of 10, and then up to 100.
Finally, add the two jumps together.

+4   +80

16   20   100

+84

16   100

|

Space Invaders

6 0

32

68
+ 23
91

Guide the aliens to the correct spaceship. You need to make 100 each time.

100

23

77

9   91

32

68

66

Dragon Danger

Help the knight pick the correct shield to make 100.

Handwritten working: 45 + 65 = 110

Shields: 45, 55 (circled), 65

Knight's card: 45

Jurassic Jump

How big a jump does the dinosaur need to make?

Handwritten working: 100 − 56 = 44   56 + 44 = 100

Jump: 44

Platforms: 56, 100

Pyramid Puzzle

Work out each missing number to make an addition equalling 100

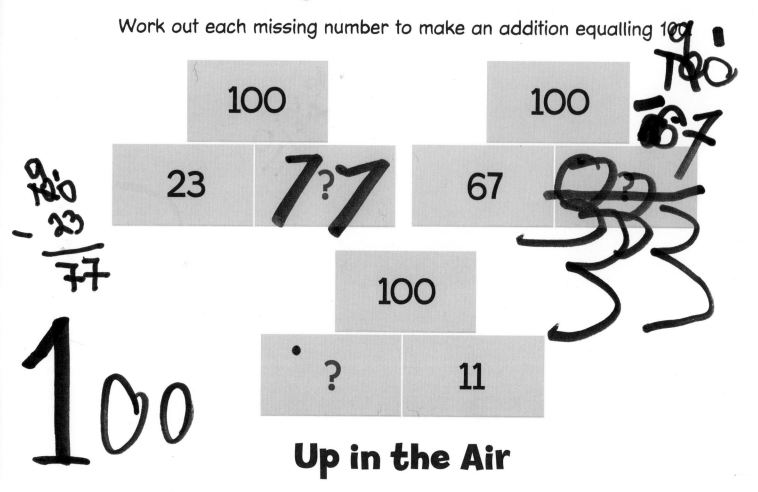

100

| 23 | ?7 |

100

| 67 | ? |

100

| ? | 11 |

(handwritten working:) 23, 77, 100; 100, 67, 33

Up in the Air

Which number needs to be added to each ball to make 100?

72 +?

34 +?

90 +?

Busy Bees

Help the bee get back to its hive. Follow the missing numbers to make 100 each time.

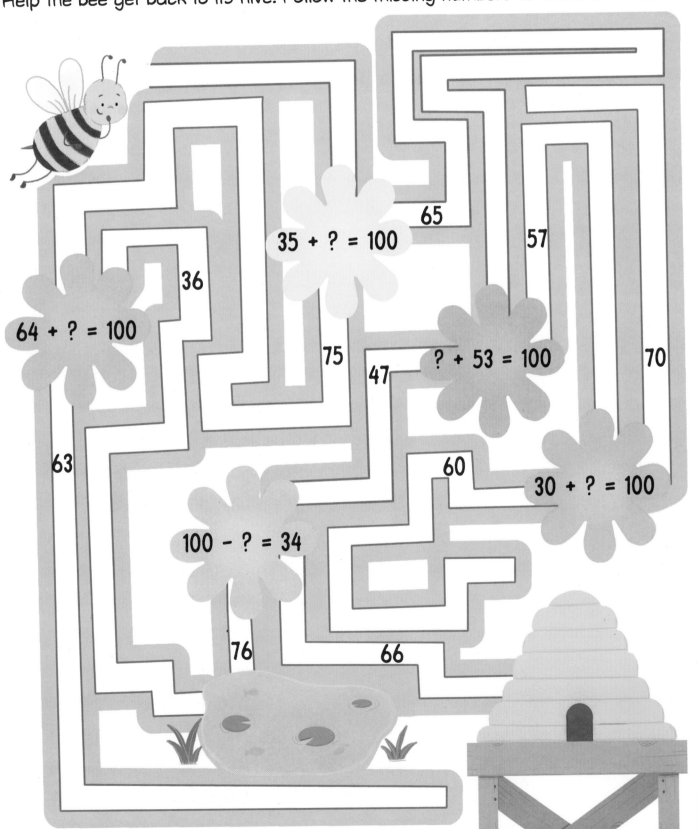

35 + ? = 100

65

57

36

64 + ? = 100

75

47

? + 53 = 100

70

63

100 − ? = 34

60

30 + ? = 100

76

66

69

Monkey Mischief

Which number is each monkey hiding?

$63 + = 100$

$100 - = 72$

$ + 36 = 100$

Amazing Astronauts

Which planet does each astronaut need to land on to make 100?

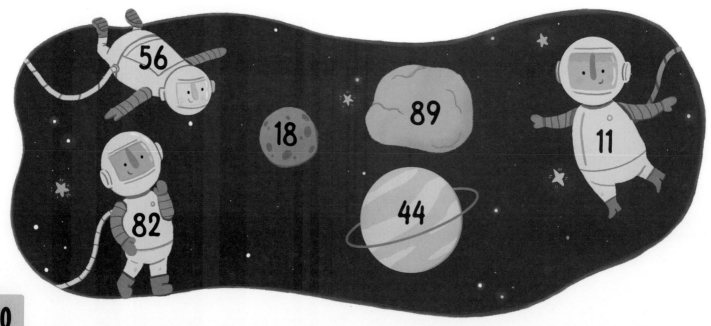

56

18

89

11

82

44

Pyramid Puzzle

Add up the two bricks next to one another to work out the value of the brick above them. The number on each brick you have worked out links to a letter.

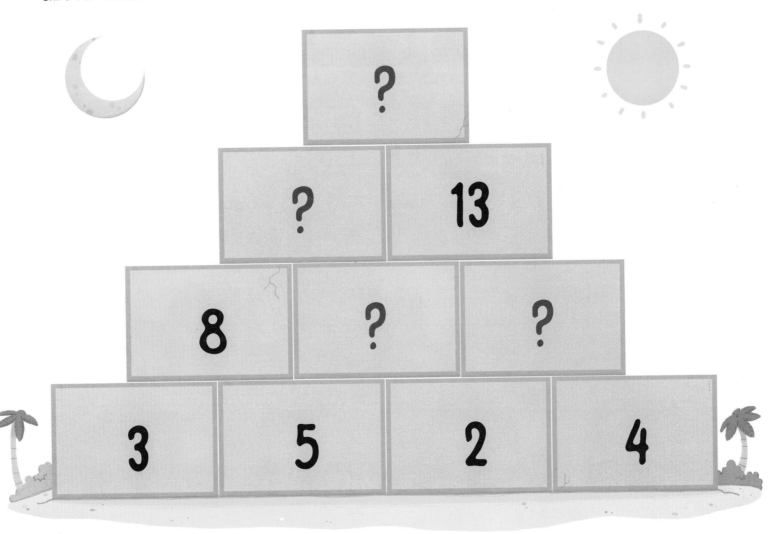

Use the key to work out what the letters are. Now jumble them around to make a word. CLUE: You have lots of them in your body!

KEY

15 = N   28 = E   27 = P

7 = B   29 = A   6 = O

_ _ _ _ _

Hundreds, Tens, and Ones: Addition

Let's try adding bigger numbers together! First, add the ones (red). Next, add the tens (blue). Then, add the hundreds (green). Finally, add the answers together!

$$324 + 415 = ?$$

$$4 + 5 = 9$$

$$20 + 10 = 30$$

$$300 + 400 = 700$$

$$700 \quad + \quad 30 \quad + \quad 9 \quad = \quad 7 \ 3 \ 9$$

Honeycomb Cover Up

Which digit is each honeycomb piece hiding?

$$538 + 361 = 8 \, \bigcirc \, 9$$

$$236 + 122 = 35 \, \bigcirc$$

$$741 + 243 = \bigcirc \, 84$$

Giddy Up!

Find the cowboy's horse.

358 + 311 = ?

669   674   623

Need for Speed

Which number is under the smoke?

651 + 316 = ?

Pick a Pirate

Which pirate has the key to the treasure?

$$482 + 515 =$$

677

997

764

Fox Trot

Match the dancing foxes up with the right partner.

849

777

948

$$555 + 222 =$$

$$636 + 312 =$$

$$632 + 217 =$$

Stuck in the Mud

Help the worm get to the apple safely. Follow the tunnel that answers each addition.

859

999

535 + 424 =

889

959

882 + 117 =

865

451

372 + 613 =

469

454

985

145 + 324 =

685

234 + 451 =

723

Monster Trucks

Help the monster pick the right road to win the race!

$652 + 246 = ?$

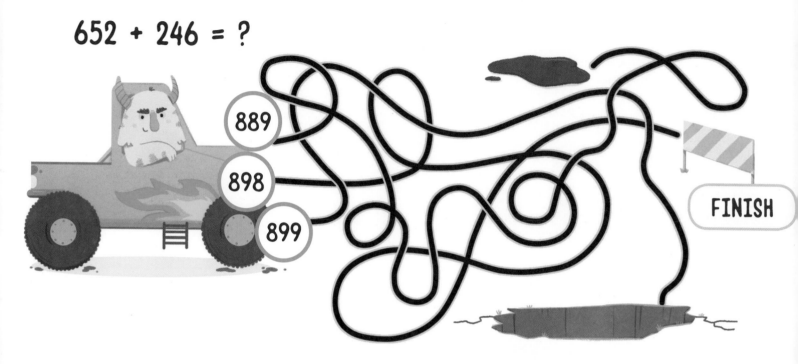

889

898

899

FINISH

Tentacle Trouble

The octopus is thinking of an addition. Draw a line to the fish with the answer.

$888 + 111 =$

999

891

998

919

819

889

919

119

Midnight Magic

Shade in the fairy.
Use the key below to help you.

372 + 625   118 + 221   567 + 121   815 + 173   467 + 111

Hundreds, Tens, and Ones: Subtraction

Now let's try it with subtraction! First, take away the ones (red). Next, take away the tens (blue). Then, take away the hundreds (green). Finally, add the answers together!

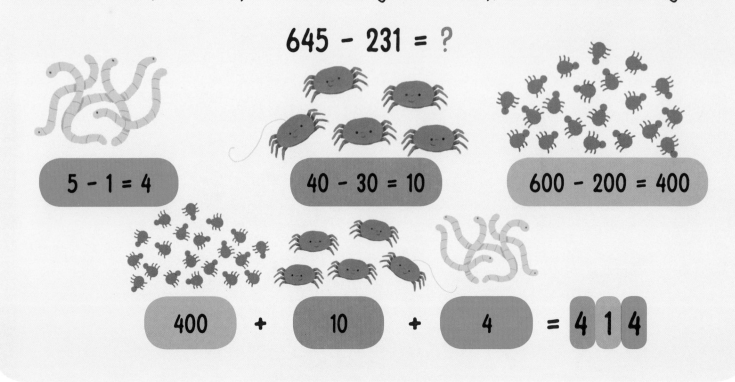

$$645 - 231 = \;?$$

5 – 1 = 4

40 – 30 = 10

600 – 200 = 400

400 + 10 + 4 = 4 1 4

Crazy Circus

Help the clown find his answer!

647 – 333 = ?

314

333

444

311

Dead Ends!

Help the racer pick the clear road!

FINISH

$859 - 436 = ?$

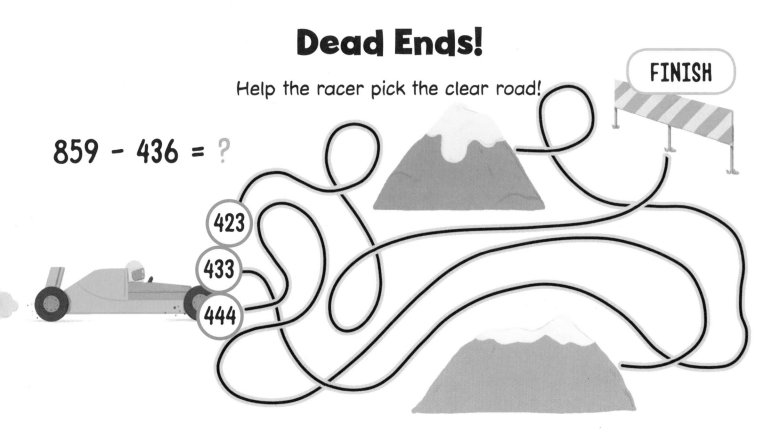

423

433

444

Undersea Sort Out

The lobster is thinking of a subtraction. Draw a line to the seahorse with the answer.

779

763

787

735

889

$888 - 111 =$

709

777

776

Paradise Lost!

Work out the answer to get rid of the cloud!

$$472 - 230 = \;?$$

What's Cooking?

Work out what is for dinner!

$$675 - 333 = \;?$$

343

342

352

Solar Sort Out

Shade in the picture. Use the key below to help you.

897-221   539-427   683-122   835-535   937-921

81

Pyramid Puzzle

Add together the bricks next to each other to work out the brick above.

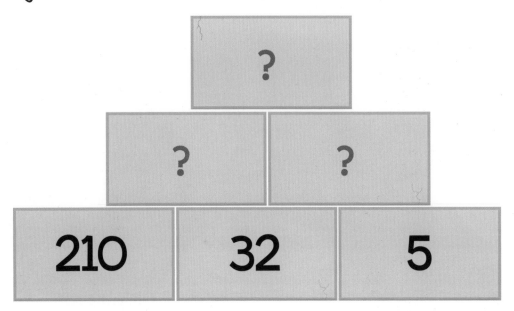

Web Worry

Work out the subtraction to help the spider find its cobweb.

893 – 771 = ?

122

142

123

FINISH

Back to the Wild

Help the animals get back home. Follow the paths with the answers to the number sentences.

322 + 20 = ?

342

876

987 − 111 = ?

332

870

60

DOUBLE 44

84

23 + 40 = ?

88

63

230

672 − 442 = ?

240

FINISH

83

Ice Work!

Keep adding 30 to help the penguin get to his friends.
Work out the missing numbers.

Doubling Dinos

Double each dinosaur's number.

The Final Battle!

Work out the magic spell to save the planet!

$$\overline{}\ \overline{}\ \overline{}\ \overline{}\ \overline{}\ \overline{}\ \overline{}\ \overline{}\ \overline{}\ \overline{}$$
1 2 3 1 4 1 5 1 2 3 1

1) 65 + 30   4) 634 + 235   869 = R   7 = D

2) Double 54   5) 898 – 756   108 = C   142 = A

3) 78 – 71   95 = B

Test Your Knowledge

Complete the number sentences.

1) 34 + 30 = ?

6) 67 - 60 = ?

2) 60 + ? = 100

7) 65 - 23 = ?

3) 73 - ? = 70

8) 20 + 120 = ?

4) 45 + 40 = ?

9) DOUBLE 25 ?

5) DOUBLE 34 ?

10) 54 - ? =10

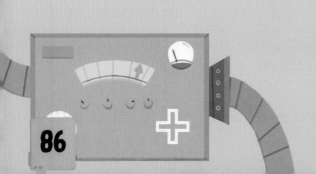

Test Your Knowledge

Complete the number sentences.

1) 35 + 20 = [?]

2) 35 [?] 20 = 15

3) 35 + [?] = 65

4) 36 + 20 = [?]

5) 65 – 5 = [?]

6) 66 – 5 = [?]

7) 100 – [?] = 66

8) 100 – [?] = 67

9) 100 – [?] = 47

10) 100 – [?] = 7

Test Your Knowledge

Complete the number sentences.

1) DOUBLE 20 ?

2) DOUBLE 22 ?

3) 22 + 22 = ?

4) 436 + 100 = ?

5) 436 + ? = 736

6) 723 + 215 = ?

7) 215 + 724 = ?

8) 574 − 133 = ?

9) 674 − 133 = ?

10) 30 + 40 + 25 = ?

88

Test Your Knowledge

Complete the number sentences.

1) 35 + 50 = ?

6) 68 – 5 = ?

2) 60 ? 20 = 40

7) 100 – ? = 66

3) 78 + ? = 100

8) 643 + 231 = ?

4) 432 + 111 = ?

9) 784 – 222 = ?

5) 65 – 5 = ?

10) 654 – 554 = ?

Solutions

Page 4   Nonsense Numbers

Page 5   Brick Fix

Page 6   Seal Surprise

2 + 3 (=) 5   5 (+) 6 = 11

6 (-) 2 = 4   20 (=) 10 + 10

Page 7   Jungle Jumble

4 (-) 6 = 10   7 (-) 3 = 10

10 (-) 5 = 15   20 (+) 5 = 15

Page 8   Magic Mix-up

6 + 5 = (11)

9 + 3 = (12)

8 + 9 = (17)

16 + 7 = (23)

Page 8   Seashell Surprise

7 + 8 = 15

Page 9   Penguin Panic

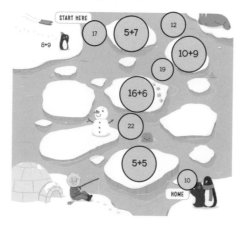

Page 10   Monster Match

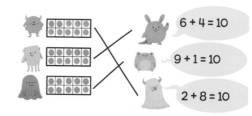

6 + 4 = 10

9 + 1 = 10

2 + 8 = 10

Page 11   Tortoise Trail

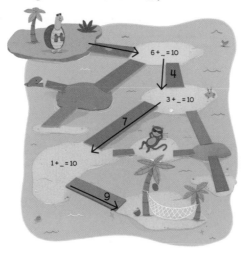

Page 12   Wild, Wild West

Page 12   Under the Sea

3 + (7) = 10

4 + 6 = (10)

(5) + 5 = 10

Page 13   Robo-road

Page 14   Pixie Party

2 + (8) = 10   5 + 5 = (10)

4 + (6) = 10   (17) + 3 = 20

9 + (11) = 20   0 + (20) = 20

Page 15   Superhero Sort Out

Page 15   Find the Treasure

18 + 2 = 20

Solutions

Page 16   Dino-roar

14 + (6) = 20
8 + (12) = 20
15 + (5) = 20
19 + (1) = 20
7 + (13) = 20

Page 16   Safari Sun

13 + 6 = (19)

Page 17   Knight Time!

11   12   18   6   16

Page 18   Test Your Knowledge

1) +   6) 12
2) +   7) 16
3) +   8) 20
4) 11   9) 20
5) 12   10) 20

Page 19   Test Your Knowledge

1) -   6) 10
2) 4   7) 15
3) -   8) 15
4) 8   9) -
5) 9   10) 7

Page 20   Balloon Brigade

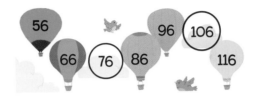

56   66   76   86   96   106   116

Page 21   Egg Run

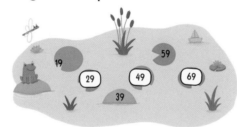

35   45   55   65   85   95   75

Page 21   Hop to It!

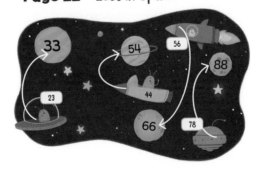

19   59   29   49   69   39

Page 22   Lost in Space

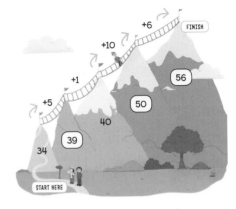

33   54   56   88   23   44   66   78

Page 22   Fox Cub Club

2 + 4 + 5 + 10 = (21)

Page 23   The Highest Heights!

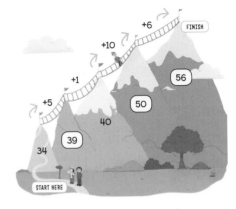

Page 24   Fire Fight!

22 + 30 = (52)
69 + 30 = (99)

Page 25   Bubble Trouble

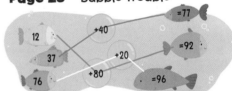

=77   +40   12   =92   37   +20   76   +80   =96

Page 25   Pyramid Puzzle

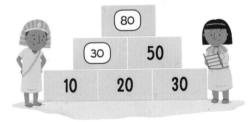

80   30   50   10   20   30

Page 26   Super Supper

67 + 30 = (97)

Page 26   Fruit Salad

4 + 6 + 40 + 13 + 7 = (70)

Solutions

Page 27   Deep Sea Diving

Page 28   Pirate Plank

Page 29   Penguin Panic!

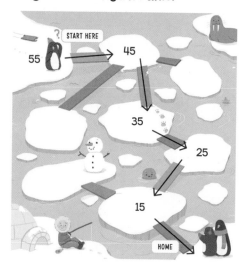

Page 30   Pick a Pride

77 - 10 = (67)

Page 30   Monkey Puzzle Trees

The two number sentences are:

67 - 10 = 57
47 - 20 = 27

Page 31   Mummy's Secret

1) 20

2) 30

3) 70

Page 32   Pyramid Puzzle

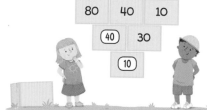

Page 33   Balloon Brigade

Page 33   Superhero Sort Out

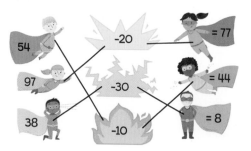

Page 34   Dino Dance

64 - 50 = (14)

Page 34   Super Save

A) 6

B) 7

C) 8

D) 2

Page 35   Back to Base Camp

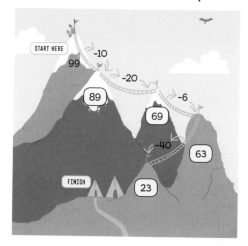

Page 36   Test Your Knowledge

1) 11   6) 65
2) 20   7) 95
3) 40   8) 99
4) 50   9) 94
5) 43   10) 100

Page 37   Test Your Knowledge

1) 1   6) 30
2) 10   7) 44
3) 20   8) 9
4) 40   9) 27
5) 43   10) 3

Solutions

Page 38   Juggle Off

Page 39   Space Stations

35 + 14 = (49)

Page 39   Tortoise Trouble

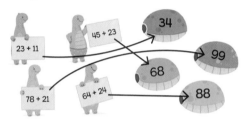

Page 40   Mermaid Mystery

C) 78 + 11 = 89

Page 40   Seal Surprise

58 − 50 = (8)

36 + 22 = (58)

Page 41   Dragon's Den

Page 42   Banana Bonanza

41 + 23 + 32 = (96)

Page 42   Rapid Repair

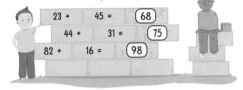

Page 43   Crack the Castle

1) 46 + 23 = 69   S

2) 82 + 16 = 98   A

3) 16 + 73 = 89   E

4) 36 + 63 = 99   L

The magic word is PLEASE.

Page 44   Picky Princess

C) 56 − 11 = 45

Page 45   Pirate Puzzle

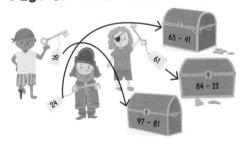

Page 45   Jungle Jumble

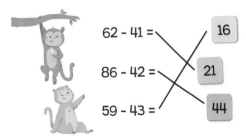

62 − 41 =   16

86 − 42 =   21

59 − 43 =   44

Page 46   Search and Rescue

68 − 41 = 27

Page 46   Bubble Burst

26 + 40 = (66)

76 − 45 = (31)

21 + 78 = (99)

Page 47   Mountain Maze

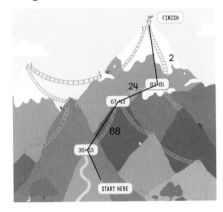

Page 48   Safari Supper

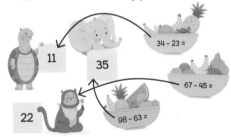

Page 48   Treasure Hunt

86 − 23 − 10 = (53)

Page 49   Crack the Code

1) 35 + 10 = (45)   N

2) 67 − 10 = (57)   I

3) 45 + 24 = (69)   B

4) 11 + 82 = (93)   L

The code word is NIBBLE.

Solutions

Page 50   Test Your Knowledge

1) 12   6) 48
2) 60   7) 6
3) 66   8) 5
4) 20   9) 20
5) 59   10) 9

Page 51   Test Your Knowledge

1) 68   6) 20
2) 88   7) 79
3) 56   8) 96
4) 22   9) 54
5) 11   10) 0

Page 52   Hop the Hurdles

B) 4   C) 8

Page 53   Washing Work Out

Page 53   Goblin Gold

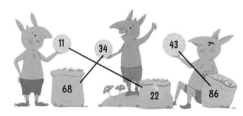

Page 54   Bingo!

73 - 30 = 43
55 - 12 = 43
33 + 10 = 43

Page 54   Pixie Party

Page 55   Showtime

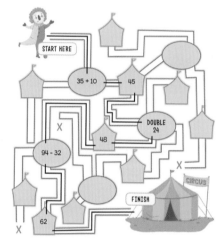

Page 56   Bug Trail

16 + 12 + 40 = 68
45 - 10 - 13 = 22
35 + 20 - 11 = 44

Page 56   Pirate Picnic

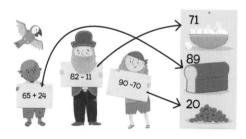

Page 57   Underwater Wonder
WELCOME

Page 58   Hard Hats On

5 + 4 = 9   9 - 5 = 4
6 + 7 = 13   13 - 6 = 7
8 + 12 = 20   20 - 8 = 12
20 + 30 = 50   50 - 20 = 30

Page 59   Balloon Brigade

40 - 30 = 10   40 - 10 = 30
30 - 10 = 20   30 - 20 = 10
70 - 40 = 30   30 - 30 = 0

Page 59   Robot Machines

45 + 11 = 56
56 - 45 = 11

Page 60   Into the Wild

9 + 57 = 66
50 - 20 = 30
14 + 34 = 48

Page 60   Wash Out

67 - 33 = 34

Page 61   Pirate Portrait

Page 62   Goblin Grab

67 - 15 = 52

Solutions

Page 62 Fairyland

46 + (53) = 99

Page 63 Mermaid Mystery

JOIN ME UNDER THE SEA

Page 64 Test Your Knowledge

1) 26   6) 2
2) 20   7) 96
3) 33   8) 41
4) 65   9) 88
5) 54   10) 4

Page 65 Test Your Knowledge

1) 4   6) 80
2) 6   7) 32
3) 8   8) 12
4) 11   9) 89
5) 40   10) 89

Page 66 Space Invaders

Page 67 Dragon Danger

45 + (55) = 100

Page 67 Jurassic Jump

56 + (44) = 100

Page 68 Pyramid Puzzle

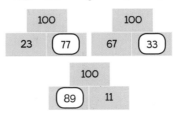

Page 68 Up in the Air

34 + (66) = 100
72 + (28) = 100
90 + (10) = 100

Page 69 Busy Bees

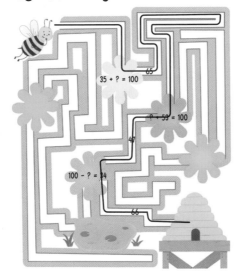

Page 70 Monkey Mischief

63 + (37) = 100
100 − (28) = 72
(64) + 36 = 100

Page 70 Amazing Astronauts

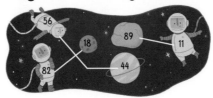

Page 70 Pyramid Puzzle

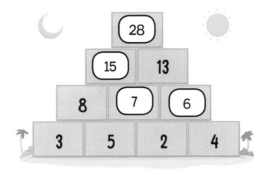

The word is BONE

Page 72 Honeycomb Cover Up

538 + 361 = (899)
236 + 122 = (358)
741 + 243 = (984)

Page 73 Giddy Up!

358 + 311 = 669

Page 73 Need for Speed

651 + 316 = 967

Page 74 Pick a Pirate

482 + 515 = 997

Page 74 Fox Trot

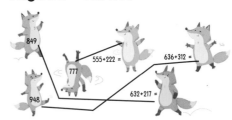

Solutions

Page 75   Stuck in the Mud

Page 76   Monster Trucks

652 + 246 = 898

Page 76   Tentacle Trouble

888 + 111 = 999

Page 77   Midnight Magic

Page 78   Crazy Circus

647 - 333 = 314

Page 79   Dead Ends!

859 - 436 = 423

Page 79   Undersea Sort Out

888 - 111 = 777

Page 80   Paradise Lost!

472 - 230 = 242

Page 80   What's Cooking?

675 - 333 = 342

Page 81   Solar Sort Out

Page 82   Pyramid Puzzle

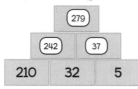

Page 82   Web Worry

893 - 771 = 122

Page 83   Back to the Wild

Page 84   Ice Work!

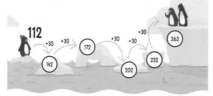

Page 84   Doubling Dinos

Page 85   The Final Battle!

The magic spell is ABRACADABRA

Page 86   Test Your Knowledge

1) 64	6) 7
2) 40	7) 42
3) 3	8) 140
4) 85	9) 50
5) 68	10) 44

Page 87   Test Your Knowledge

1) 55	6) 61
2) -	7) 34
3) 30	8) 33
4) 56	9) 53
5) 60	10) 93

Page 88   Test Your Knowledge

1) 40	6) 938
2) 44	7) 939
3) 44	8) 441
4) 536	9) 541
5) 300	10) 95

Page 89   Test Your Knowledge

1) 85	6) 63
2) -	7) 34
3) 22	8) 874
4) 543	9) 562
5) 60	10) 100